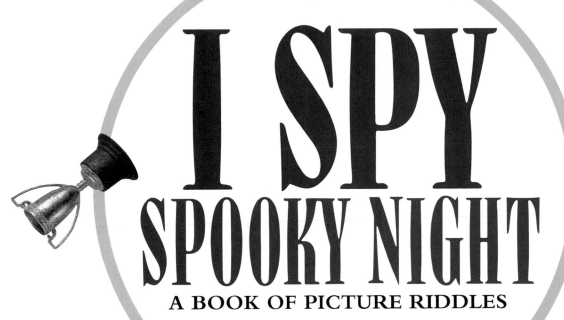

I SPY
SPOOKY NIGHT
A BOOK OF PICTURE RIDDLES

Photographs by **Walter Wick**
Riddles by **Jean Marzollo**

With new bonus challenges by
Dan Marzollo and **Dave Marzollo**

cartwheel **books**™

An imprint of Scholastic Inc.
New York

For Nathan and Matt Goodell
W.W.

For Luisa, Lily, and Julia
J.M.

Book design by Carol Devine Carson

Text copyright © 1996 by Jean Marzollo
Photographs copyright © 1996 by Walter Wick
Bonus challenges copyright © 2019 by Dan Marzollo and Dave Marzollo
Library of Congress Cataloging-in-Publication Data available
ISBN 978-1-338-35313-6
10 9 8 7 6 5   21 22 23
Printed in China   62
This edition first printing, August 2019

TABLE OF CONTENTS

....

Picture riddles fill this book;
Turn the pages! Take a look!

Use your mind, use your eye;
Read the riddles—play I SPY!

....

I spy a broken bone and — BOO!
A padlock and 1892;

A train, a chain, a busted seam,
An eye of stone, and a silent SCREAM.

I spy four pumpkins, a ruler, a bat,
Eight pinecones, a ladder, three acorns, a cat;

A scarecrow, a key, a clothespin, a clock,
Two bowling pins, and KNOCK, KNOCK, KNOCK!

I spy a swan, a turtle, a bear,
A lizard, MOM, and a bone repair;

Four owls, a yardstick, a spool, a comb,
BEWARE, a mouse, and ANYBODY HOME?

I spy a beetle, a snake in the grass,
One dozen ants, two birdies of brass;

Eight hands, a frog, a seafaring bird,
A spider, twin ducks, and a backward word.

I spy a crayon, a dinosaur lamp,
TICK TOCK TICK, an eagle, a stamp;

Three nails, three springs, a wishbone, a four,
And a string that hangs from a hidden door.

I spy an X, four spiders, a cat,
Two kids with a dog, WORKSHOP, a bat;

A candle that's old, a candle that's new,
And a big red box with a rebus clue.

I spy a shark, three bats, and a map,
Two paddles, an anchor, a red bottle cap;

An egg that is cracked, a rabbit, a three,
A bowling pin stone, and a skeleton key.

I spy a clothespin, a short sad poem,
A magnet, a mouse, a little palindrome;

Three corks, a spool, a black cat spout,
A whistle, a wagon, a whale, and WATCH OUT!

I spy a ladder, pliers, a nail,
Three fish, a swan, and a ghostly sail;

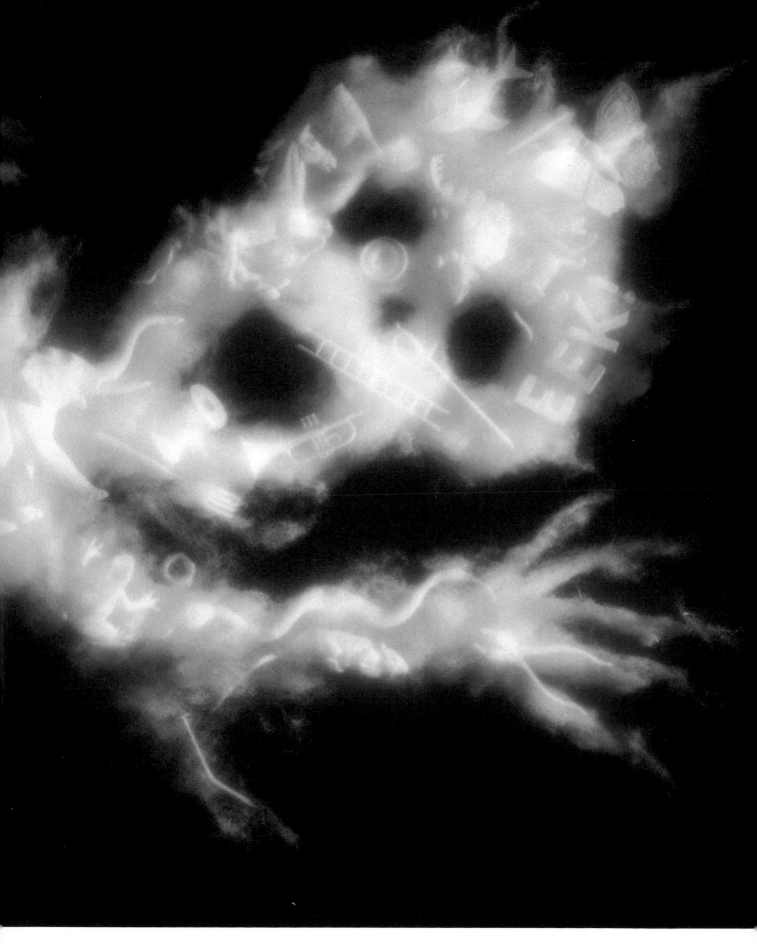

A trumpet, a shovel, an ostrich beak,
Two mice, a sword, a snake, and EEK!

I spy an owl, a lizard, a mouse,
A spider, three swans, a pig, a house;

A knife, a fork, an apple, some rope,
A race car, a shoe, and a brass telescope.

I spy a saddle, six rabbits, a rose,
A seahorse, a windmill, and two dominoes;

Nine birds, a paintbrush, a little blue bow;
A feather, a fan, and an old radio.

I spy a knight, a lion, a dime,
A spoon, a moon, and ONCE upon a TIME.

A cat with stripes, a key on a chair,
Two robots, a phone, and ENTER IF YOU DARE.

BONUS CHALLENGES

by Dan Marzollo and Dave Marzollo

"Find Me" Riddle

In every picture I'm having fun.
I'm a spooky _____ !

There are still more riddles for you to complete.
Here is a challenge for readers to beat!

Every picture has a new set of clues.
Can you pick the right page to choose?

I spy a bell, a pink fish, a rainbow,
A car that's fast, and a wagon that's slow.

I spy a watering can, a half baseball,
Eight clothespins, a snake, and a frog on a wall.

I spy three nails, a small lion head,
A sword, and an arrow that's pointing to red.

I spy a teacup, a shirt that is blue,
Smoke, a wheel, a striped tail, and YOU.

I spy a swan, an owl, CANOE,
A skunk, an X, and a little horseshoe.

I spy a mask, two basket handles,
A lantern, a goose, and three tiny candles.

I spy a trumpet, four fish, a star,
A bee, a trophy, and a little guitar.

I spy a fork, a hole for a mouse,
Scissors, a spider, and a tree that's a house.

I spy two skulls, a dog that's white,
A table, a turtle, and a traffic light.

I spy a penny, a goose, a bat,
A tack, pliers, and a gentleman's hat.

I spy a key, a gear, a pail,
A saw, a spool, and a spiky tail.

I spy a pinecone, a chimney, a bell,
A frog, a mouse, a key, and a shell.

What Is a Rebus? A Palindrome?

In a rebus, pictures stand for words — for example, an eyeball for "I," a heart for "love," and a U for "you." A palindrome reads the same backward and forward — for example, WOW.

Write Your Own Spooky Stories

What scary stories can you make up to go with the pictures in this book? Use your imagination. There are no "right" answers — so be creative! Try telling the story from four different points of view: the person entering the haunted house, the skeleton, the original owner of the house, and the child who owns the dollhouse.

How *I Spy Spooky Night* Was Made

Walter Wick created the elaborate sets for *I Spy Spooky Night* in his studio and then photographed them with an 8" by 10" view camera. The sets vary in size. Clues to their actual dimensions are provided by ordinary objects and toys: a baseball, a yardstick, a candle, a crayon. To make the haunted house, Mr. Wick altered a Victorian dollhouse. He lit the interior and painted a spooky sky for a backdrop. The gates, the rooms, and the outside scenes were carefully constructed with wood, STYROFOAM, cloth, toys, dry ice, cotton, household objects, and dollhouse props.

The spooky tree in the graveyard shot was made from a blueberry bush, to which Mr. Wick added and subtracted branches until he achieved the dramatic look he wanted. Each finished set was lit by Mr. Wick to create the right shadows, depth, and mood. When the final photograph was made, the set was dismantled.

Acknowledgments

We extend a special thanks to Bruce Morozko for his artistry, expertise, and help in the construction of the sets of "The Empty Hall," "A Blazing Fire," "The Library," "Discovery in the Graveyard," and "The Fountain." We are grateful for the patience and dedication of Dan Helt, Walter Wick's assistant throughout the entire project, and for the contributions of Lee Hitt, Krista Borst, Maria McGowan, Rick Schwab, The Torrington Doll House, and the unfailing support of Linda Cheverton-Wick. We appreciate the assistance of Grace Maccarone, Bernette Ford, Edie Weinberg, and Angela Biola. Lastly, we thank our agent Molly Friedrich at Aaron Priest Agency for her wise guidance.

Walter Wick and Jean Marzollo

Jean Marzollo

Award-winning author Jean Marzollo was the author of over a hundred books, including the bestselling I Spy series; *Help Me Learn Numbers 0–20*; *Help Me Learn Addition*; *Help Me Learn Subtraction*; *Pierre the Penguin*; *Soccer Sam*; *Happy Birthday, Martin Luther King*; *The Little Plant Doctor*; *In 1776*; *Mama Mama/Papa Papa*; and *I Am Water*; as well as books for parents and teachers, such as *The New Kindergarten*. As a child, Jean loved to read and make dolls' clothes. She grew up in Manchester, Connecticut, and graduated from the University of Connecticut and Harvard Graduate School of Education. Her sons, Dan and Dave, helped Jean write some of the newer I Spy books. Jean made sure that every riddle in every I Spy book was rich with concrete words that children could understand and that those words were set in an inviting pattern of rhythm and rhyme. "We are hunters and gatherers," she said. "Kids love the challenge of even the very hardest things in Walter Wick's brilliant and beautiful photographs." For more information, go to scholastic.com/ispy.

How the I Spy Books Were Made

Jean Marzollo and Walter Wick together conceived the ideas for the I Spy books. As sets were constructed, they conferred on objects to go in the pictures, selecting things for their rhyming potential, as well as their aesthetic, playful, and educational qualities. The final riddles were written upon completion of the photographs.

Walter Wick

Walter Wick is the award-winning photographer of the I Spy series as well as the author and photographer of the bestselling Can You See What I See? series. Walter has loved to tinker and invent ever since he was a child. After graduating from Paier College of Art, he soon developed a reputation as an ingenious photographic illustrator. In addition to illustrating posters for *Let's Find Out* and covers for *Newsweek*, *Psychology Today*, and *Discover*, Walter invented numerous photographic puzzles for *GAMES* magazine. After creating the photographic puzzles for the first I Spy book in 1991, Walter found the perfect audience for his unique vision. He has been creating acclaimed children's books ever since. His other books include *A Drop of Water: A Book of Science and Wonder*, which won numerous awards, including the Boston Globe–Horn Book Award for Nonfiction. His book *Walter Wick's Optical Tricks* was named a Best Illustrated Children's Book by the *New York Times Book Review* and a Notable Children's Book by the American Library Association, in addition to many other awards. Walter lives in Florida with his wife, Linda. More information about Walter Wick is available at walterwick.com and scholastic.com/canyouseewhatisee.

Carol Devine Carson, the book designer for the first I Spy books, is art director at Alfred A. Knopf Publishers. She has designed covers for books by John Updike, Joan Didion, Alice Munro, Bill Clinton, and Pope John Paul II. For nineteen years, Marzollo and Carson produced Scholastic's kindergarten magazine, *Let's Find Out*.